Baby Animals

Heather Hammonds

NELSON

★

THOMSON LEARNING

Australia · Canada · Mexico · Singapore · Spain · United Kingdom · United States

Hop, hop, hop,

goes the kangaroo.

Inside her pouch

is a joey, too!

See me swing
from tree to tree.
My little baby
swings with me.

4

This bird keeps

her little chicks

safe inside

a nest of sticks.

Come, little baby,
come ride with me.
Come, little baby,
we will sit in a tree.

With her long legs
and neck,
she's not so small.
This baby giraffe
will grow very tall!

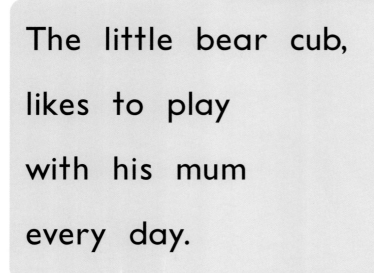

The little bear cub,

likes to play

with his mum

every day.

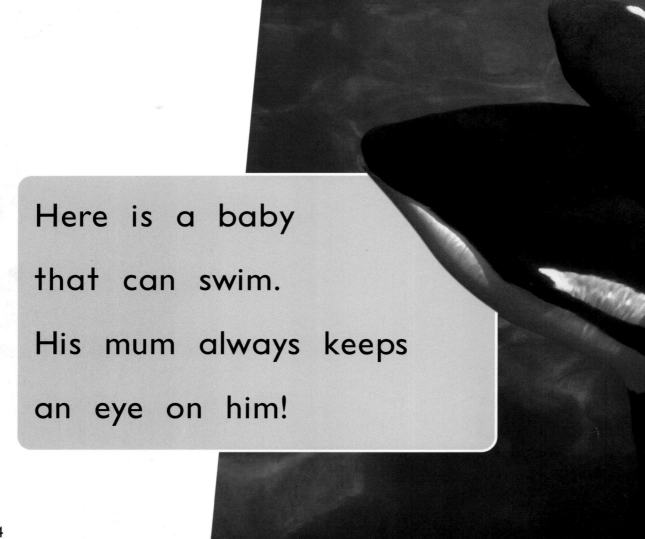

Here is a baby
that can swim.
His mum always keeps
an eye on him!

Babies, babies,

look at them all!

Baby animals,

big and small!